波波唸翻天系列 3

波波上課記

Justine Korman　著

Lucinda McQueen　繪

本局編輯部　譯

三民書局

For Patsy Jensen, an editor who's never grumpy
—J.K.

獻給派奇・傑森，一位永不抱怨的編輯
—J.K.

For Abby Guitar —Lots of love from Aunt Lucy

獻給愛比・吉塔 — 好多好多的愛，來自露西阿姨

Hopper woke up to a perfect September day. Orange and gold leaves **twirled** in the **fresh** fall **breeze**. The sky was a bright, clear blue.

But Hopper felt grumpy. **In fact**, the grumpy bunny was even grumpier than usual because today was the first day of school.

這是個完美的九月天，波波從睡夢中醒來。橘色和金黃色的樹葉在涼爽的秋風中打轉。天空很耀眼，一片明亮的湛藍。

但是波波感到悶悶不樂。事實上，這隻愛抱怨的兔子跟平時比起來牢騷更多，因為今天是上課的第一天。

Once again, Hopper would be helping Mrs. Clover teach
the kinderbunny class at Easter Bunny **Elementary School**.
That was where young bunnies went to learn how to be Easter
Bunnies.

波波又要去幫克拉佛太太教復活節兔寶寶小學裡的幼幼班了。兔寶寶們在那兒學習如何
成為復活節兔寶寶。

The new bunnies were always every **excited**. But to Hopper, school was just the same old ho-hum, humdrum thing.

新來的兔寶寶總是非常興奮。可是對波波來說，上課就是一成不變的無聊事情。

一開始，兔寶寶們會繞著大樹圍成一圈，然後，復活節兔寶寶的領袖，兔老爹拜倫先生就會帶領他們讀復活節兔寶寶的宣誓詞：

First the bunnies would **gather** around the Great Tree while the **chief** of all the Easter Bunnies, Sir Byron the Great Hare, would lead them in the Easter Bunny's **Pledge**:

*Making **treats** with care and art,*
Bringing love to every heart,
***Spreading** sunshine every day,*
That's the Easter Bunny way!

用心與雙手做小點心，
把愛帶給每一顆心，
讓陽光散播在每一天，
復活節兔寶寶永不改變。

Then all the eager, **scared**, happy young bunnies would hop off to their classes. Mrs. Clover always started the day with egg coloring. She taught the same **patterns** every year: **straight** lines and flowers, all just so. Then came marshmallow **puffing** and basket **weaving**.

接著，所有熱切的、害怕的、快樂的兔寶寶們就會蹦蹦地跳到他們的教室。克拉佛太太總是以教畫彩蛋開始課程。她每年都教畫相同的圖案：直線與花朵。接著是吹雪棉糖和編籃子。

The three-**carrot snack** would be followed by a nap, then
hippety-hop drills, wheelbarrow practice, and, finally, treat
hiding.

吃完三根紅蘿蔔點心後，接著小睡一下，然後練習蹦蹦跳、推獨輪車，最後是藏點心。

Hopper sighed. It was time to go. In fact, the first schoolbunnies were already gathering around the Great Tree as Hopper dragged himself down the **path** to school. His poor feet felt very tired.

How will I ever get through all those boring hippety-hop drills? he **wondered miserably**.

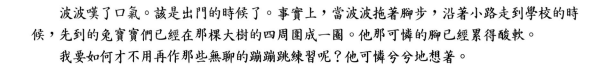
波波嘆了口氣。該是出門的時候了。事實上,當波波拖著腳步,沿著小路走到學校的時候,先到的兔寶寶們已經在那棵大樹的四周圍成一圈。他那可憐的腳已經累得酸軟。
我要如何才不用再作那些無聊的蹦蹦跳練習呢?他可憐兮兮地想著。

Hopper reached the Great Tree just as the schoolbunnies were finishing the pledge. He put his **paw** over his heart and **muttered**, "Spreading sunshine, and all that ho-hum, humdrum."

波波走到那棵大樹的時候，兔寶寶們正好要完成宣誓。他把手掌放在心口上，喃喃地說，「讓陽光散播，呵──好無聊。」

Suddenly Hopper **realized** Sir Byron was looking right at him!
"I'm sorry I was late," Hopper began.
But Sir Byron said, "No time for that now. You've got a class to teach. Mrs. Clover is sick. You're on your own today."

忽然，波波發現拜倫先生正盯著他瞧！
「對不起，我遲到了。」波波開始說道。
但是拜倫先生告訴他說，「現在沒有時間說抱歉。有個班要讓你來教。克拉佛太太病了。今天要靠你自己了。」

Hopper's ears flew up in surprise. "What? That's not **fair**!" he started to **complain**. Then Hopper had an idea.

"Well, **perhaps** I could get someone else..." Sir Byron began.

But Hopper shook his head. "Never mind, sir. I'll be fine." And he hopped off before the Great Hare could wonder why the grumpy bunny wasn't being grumpy anymore.

波波驚訝地豎起了耳朵。「什麼？那不公平！」他開始抱怨。然後波波想到了一個點子。

「嗯！或許我可以找別人……」拜倫先生開始說道。

但是波波搖了搖頭。「沒關係，先生，我沒問題。」波波說完便轉身蹦蹦地離開了，兔老爹一下子搞不清楚，為什麼這隻愛抱怨的兔子今天不再有滿腹的牢騷。

Hopper hopped **toward** the kinderbunny room. *Today I can do things my way!* he thought happily.

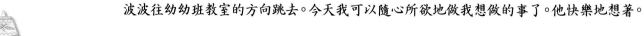

波波往幼幼班教室的方向跳去。今天我可以隨心所欲地做我想做的事了。他快樂地想著。

And that's just what Hopper did! First he painted the craziest-looking egg anyone had ever seen.

Then Hopper told the kinderbunnies, "Paint your eggs however you want. Just make them as pretty as you can."

我們來看波波到底做了些什麼！首先，他畫了一個有史以來最古怪的彩蛋。

然後波波告訴兔寶寶們，「你們想要怎麼畫彩蛋就怎麼畫吧！盡量把它們畫得漂漂亮亮的。」

"The kinderbunnies went far **beyond stripes** and flowers. They painted **designs** Hopper had never even imagined. There were **star-spangled** eggs, rainbow eggs, and eggs with **leopard** spots. One even **grinned** like a bright orange **jack-o'-lantern**.

這些兔寶寶不再只是畫線條和花朵。他們畫出了連波波都想像不到的圖案。

有的是閃亮的小星星、有的是彩虹、有的是豹紋斑點。有一個蛋甚至被畫成一顆咧嘴微笑的鮮橙色南瓜燈籠。

波波沒有規定籃子的形狀。反而只給兔寶寶們一些稻草。

Hopper didn't **hand out** patterns for the baskets. Instead, he just gave the kinderbunnies pieces of **straw** and said, "Weave the baskets however you want. The colors and shapes are **up to** you. Just make them as beautiful as you can."

然後說道，「這些籃子你們愛怎麼編就怎麼編。顏色和形狀都由你們決定。只要盡量做漂亮一點就可以了。」

When it came time for the marshmallow puffing, Hopper didn't make the usual speech about being careful not to puff too much. He decided to let the kinderbunnies find out for themselves.

PUFF, PUFF, they puffed up their **chicks**...

...till one bunny named Peter puffed too much. *PA-WUFFFF!* Marshmallow went flying everywhere!

吹雪棉糖的時間到了，波波沒有說一些要他們小心不要吹太用力那種老掉牙的話。他決定讓兔寶寶們自己去嘗試。

噗，噗，他們吹出了自己的小雞……

……結果有一隻叫彼得的兔寶寶吹進太多氣。

啪——呼！雪棉糖濺得到處都是！

"Let's all do that!" the other bunnies **shrieked** happily.

"All right," Hopper said. "But see if you can tell **exactly** when the chick is about to **explode**. That way you'll learn how much puffing is too much."

「我們都那樣做吧！」其他的兔寶寶興奮地尖叫。

「好吧！」波波說，「但是注意哦！看你們能不能拿捏得準小雞何時會破掉。那樣你們就會知道吹到多大才是剛剛好了。」

A few minutes later, Hopper asked the **sticky** bunnies to gather together. "You all know how to hippety-hop," he began. "Now try to hoppety-hip. Because once you can hoppety-hip, hippety-hopping is a **snap**."

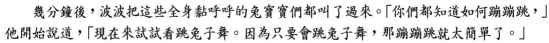

幾分鐘後，波波把這些全身黏呼呼的兔寶寶們都叫了過來。「你們都知道如何蹦蹦跳，」他開始說道，「現在來試試看跳兔子舞。因為只要會跳兔子舞，那蹦蹦跳就太簡單了。」

"It's hard," a kinderbunny named Daisy said.
"No, it's fun!" cried her friend Flopsy.

「好難哦，」一隻叫黛絲的兔寶寶說。
「不會啊，這很好玩！」她的朋友晃晃叫道。

When the bunnies **were tired of** hoppety-hipping, Hopper said, "Every Easter Bunny must learn to push a wheelbarrow filled with treats. We could **march** our wheelbarrows **back and forth** across the room—or we could have a race!"

The kinderbunnies **cheered**. Soon they were racing around the room, laughing with **glee**.

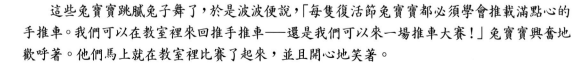

這些兔寶寶跳膩兔子舞了，於是波波便說，「每隻復活節兔寶寶都必須學會推載滿點心的手推車。我們可以在教室裡來回推手推車——還是我們可以來一場推車大賽！」兔寶寶興奮地歡呼著。他們馬上就在教室裡比賽了起來，並且開心地笑著。

Just then Sir Byron **appeared**. "What's all this noise?"
shouted the Great Hare.

Every bunny fell silent. Hopper's ears **dropped** and his
stomach **flippety-flopped**. "Um, I..." the nervous bunny
stammered.

就在這個時候，拜倫先生出現了。「你們在吵什麼？」兔老爹大喊。

所有的兔寶寶都安靜下來。波波的耳朵垂了下來，他的胃在翻絞著。「嗯，我……」他緊
張得連說話都結巴了。

"We were having a wheelbarrow race!" shouted Flopsy.

One look at Sir Byron's angry face and Hopper knew he was in deep trouble. He looked down at his **sore** feet and wished he'd never gotten out of bed.

Sir Byron looked around the marshmallow-**strewn** room. "What's all this **mess**?" he asked.

Hopper didn't know what to say. "I...we..."

"We made our chicks so puffy they exploded!" Peter cried. *"PA-WUFFFF!"* he **added**, puffing up his **furry** cheeks.

「我們正在比賽推車！」晃晃叫道。一看到拜倫先生生氣的臉，波波就知道他的麻煩大了。他低頭看著疼痛的雙腳。早知道就不要起床了。拜倫先生環顧沾滿雪棉糖汁的教室。

「這裡亂糟糟的是怎麼回事啊？」他問道。波波不知道該說什麼。「我……我們……」

「我們把雪棉糖吹得太大，結果把它們都吹爆了！」彼得叫道。「啪──呼！」他鼓起毛絨絨的腮幫子，又叫了一聲。

Hopper **groaned**. This day was getting worse by the minute.

Then Sir Byron **spotted** the eggs drying on the **windowsill**. "And what happened here? Did you forget to show them the proper painting patterns?"

Daisy said, "Hopper let us paint whatever we wanted. It was fun!"

"I see," said the Great Hare. Then he stared at the eggs. "Some of these are actually quite pretty."

Hopper's ears lifted. Had he heard Sir Byron right?

波波抱怨了起來。今天真是越過越慘了。

然後拜倫先生瞧見放在窗臺上晾乾的彩蛋。「這又是怎麼回事？你忘了給他們看正確的彩繪圖案嗎？」黛絲說，「波波讓我們想怎麼畫就怎麼畫。真好玩！」「我明白了，」兔老爹說。然後他盯著那些蛋看。「有幾顆蛋確實是很漂亮。」波波的耳朵豎了起來。他沒聽錯拜倫先生的話吧？

"**Tradition** is good. But there's always room for new ideas," the Great Hare **declared**. "A wheelbarrow race might help **improve** their skills—and the bunnies certainly seemed to enjoy it. And perhaps letting the bunnies explode a few marshmallows is the best way to teach them when to stop puffing," the Great Hare added.

Hopper's jaw dropped. Sir Byron **clapped** him on the back. "You'll make a fine teacher someday, Hopper. In the future, though, I hope you'll bring your ideas to me first."

「傳統是很好。但是也有發揮創意的空間，」兔老爹肯定地說。他又補充說，「推車比賽應該有助於改善他們的技巧──而且兔寶寶們似乎真的玩得很開心。另外，或許教兔寶寶們吹糖，最好的方法就是讓他們吹破一些雪棉糖。」

波波驚訝得連嘴巴都合不起來了。拜倫先生拍拍他的背，「波波，有一天你會成為一位好老師的。但是我希望以後你先把你的點子告訴我。」

Hopper **nodded** eagerly. He still couldn't quite believe that he wasn't in trouble.

"Of course, you'll have to **clean up** this mess," the Great Hare said.

Hopper's heart **sank**. It would take him all afternoon to clean up the sticky room.

波波急忙點了點頭。他還是不太敢相信自己竟然沒事。

「當然啦，你必須把這裡清乾淨，」兔老爹說。

波波的心往下沈。打掃這間黏呼呼的教室可得花上他一整個下午的時間。

Then Daisy said, "We'll help you, Hopper."

"Yes!" Flopsy cried. "You're our **favorite** teacher!"

"Even cleaning up will be fun with you!" Peter declared. And, to Hopper's **amazement**, it was.

然後黛絲說，「波波，我們會幫你的。」
「對呀！」晃晃叫道，「你是我們最喜歡的老師！」
「只要和你一起，就算是打掃，也會很好玩！」彼得說道。
而且，波波驚訝地發現到，那一點兒也沒錯。

Hopper hippety-hopped all the way home. He was so happy that even his sore feet felt good!

波波一路輕快地跳回家去。他好高興，甚至連疼痛的雙腳也覺得舒服了！

Back in his burrow, Hopper decided, "Tomorrow I'll ask Sir Byron if I can teach jellybean juggling."

He couldn't wait to go back to school the next day. In fact, from that day on, Hopper was never grumpy about going to school again.

回到他的地下小窩裡，波波下定決心，「明天我要問問拜倫先生，看他願不願意讓我教拋QQ豆的技巧。」

他等不及明天要回學校去。事實上，從那一天起，波波就不再抱怨上課的事了。

clap [klæp] 動 拍打，輕拍
clean up 打掃
complain [kəm`plen] 動 抱怨

add [æd] 動 附加
amazement [ə`mezmənt] 名 驚奇
appear [ə`pɪr] 動 出現

back and forth 來回地
be tired of 對…感到厭煩
beyond [bɪ`jɑnd] 介 遠於…，超過
breeze [briz] 名 微風

carrot [`kærət] 名 胡蘿蔔
cheer [tʃɪr] 動 歡呼
chick [tʃɪk] 名 小雞
chief [tʃif] 名 領袖

declare [dɪ`klɛr] 動 聲明
design [dɪ`zaɪn] 名 圖案
drill [drɪl] 名 訓練，練習
drop [drɑp] 動 垂下，掉落

elementary school 小學
exactly [ɪg`zæktlɪ] 副 精確地
excited [ɪk`saɪtɪd] 形 興奮的
explode [ɪk`splod] 動 爆炸

fair [fɛr] 形 公平的

favorite [`fevrɪt] 形 最喜愛的

flippety-flop 動 翻滾

fresh [frɛʃ] 形 涼爽的，新鮮的

furry [`fɝɪ] 形 披有毛皮的

jack-o'-lantern [`dʒækə,læntən] 名 南瓜燈籠

gather [`gæðə] 動 聚集

glee [gli] 名 歡喜

grin [grɪn] 動 露齒微笑

groan [gron] 動 抱怨

leopard [`lɛpəd] 名 豹

march [mɑrtʃ] 動 前進，行進

mess [mɛs] 名 雜亂，亂七八糟

miserably [`mɪzrəblɪ] 副 可憐地，不幸地

mutter [`mʌtə] 動 輕聲低語

hand out 分發，分配

hippety-hop 名 動 跳躍

nod [nɑd] 動 點頭

improve [ɪm`pruv] 動 改善

in fact 事實上

path [pæθ] 名 小徑

pattern [`pætɚn] 名 花樣，圖案

paw [pɔ] 名 動物的腳掌

perhaps [pɚ`hæps] 副 或許，可能

pledge [plɛdʒ] 名 誓約，誓言

puff [pʌf] 動 吹（氣）

realize [`rɪə‚laɪz] 動 理解，認清

scared [skɛrd] 形 受驚嚇的

shriek [ʃrik] 動 尖聲說

sink [sɪŋk] 動 下沈（過去式 sank）

snack [snæk] 名 小吃，點心

snap [snæp] 名 輕而易舉的事

sore [sɔr] 形 痛的

spot [spat] 動 發現

spread [sprɛd] 動 散佈

stammer [`stæmɚ] 動 口吃，結巴

star-spangled [`star‚spæŋgld] 形 布滿星星的

sticky [`stɪkɪ] 形 黏的

straight [stret] 形 直線的

straw [strɔ] 名 稻草

strew [stru] 動 撒落

stripe [straɪp] 名 線條

toward [tord] 介 向…，朝…

tradition [trə`dɪʃən] 名 傳統

treat [trit] 名 小點心

twirl [twɝl] 動 旋轉，轉動

up to 由…的意思而決定

weave [wiv] 動 編織

windowsill [`wɪndo͵sɪl] 名 窗臺

wonder [`wʌndɚ] 動 納悶，想知道

精心規劃，內容詳盡
三民英漢辭典系列
學習英文的最佳輔助工具

三民皇冠英漢辭典（革新版）

大學教授、中學老師一致肯定、推薦！
最適合中學生和英語初學者使用的實用辭典！

◎ 明顯標示國中生必學的507個單字和最常犯的錯誤，詳細、淺顯、易懂！
◎ 收錄豐富詞條及例句，幫助您輕鬆閱讀課外讀物！
◎ 詳盡的「參考」及「印象」欄，讓您體會英語的「弦外之音」！
◎ 賞心悅目的雙色印刷及趣味橫生的插圖，讓查閱辭典成為一大享受！

三民新知英漢辭典

一本很生活、很實用的英漢辭典！
讓您在生動、新穎的解說中快樂學習！

◎收錄中學、大專所需詞彙43,000字，總詞目多達60,000項。
◎增列「同義字圖表」，使同義字字義及用法差異在圖解說明下，一目了然。
◎加強重要字彙多義性的「用法指引」，充份掌握主要用法及用例。
◎雙色印刷，編排醒目；插圖生動靈活，加強輔助理解字義。

中學生・大專生適用

多種選擇，多種編寫設計
三民英漢辭典系列
最能符合你的需要

三民精解英漢辭典（革新版）

一本真正賞心悅目、趣味橫生的英漢辭典誕生了！
雙色印刷＋漫畫式插圖，保證讓您愛不釋手！

◎收錄詞條25,000字，以中學生、社會人士常用詞彙為主。
◎常用基本字彙以較大字體標示，並搭配豐富的使用範例。
◎以五大句型為基礎，讓您更容易活用動詞型態。
◎豐富的漫畫式插圖，讓您在快樂的氣氛中學習，促進學習效率。
◎以圖框對句法結構、語法加以詳盡解說。

中學生・初學者適用

三民新英漢辭典（增訂完美版）

◎收錄詞目增至67,500字（詞條增至46,000項）。
◎新增「搭配」欄，羅列常用詞語間的組合關係，讓您掌握英語的慣用搭
　配，說出道地的英語。
◎詳列原義、引申義，確實掌握字詞釋義，加強英語字彙的活用能力。
◎附有精美插圖千餘幅，輔助詞義理解。
◎附錄包括詳盡的「英文文法總整理」、「發音要領解說」，提升學習效率。
◎雙色印刷，並附彩色英美地圖及世界地圖。

中學生・大專生適用

~ 看的繪本＋聽的繪本　童話小天地最能捉住孩子的心 ~

為孩子寫～彩色的夢

 兒童文學叢書

·童話小天地·

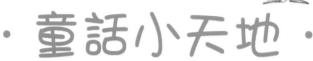

○ 奇妙的紫貝殼
簡 宛·文　朱美靜·圖

○ 奇奇的磁鐵鞋
林黛嫚·文　黃子瑄·圖

○ 九重葛笑了
陳 冷·文　吳佩蓁·圖

○ 智慧市的糊塗市民
劉靜娟·文　郜欣／倪靖·圖

○ 銀毛與斑斑
李民安·文　廖健宏·圖

○ 丁伶郎
潘人木·文
鄭凱軍／羅小紅·圖

○ 屋頂上的祕密
劉靜娟·文　郝洛玟·圖

○ 石頭不見了
李民安·文　翱 子·圖

嗨～神奇寶貝、酷斯拉都靠邊站，爸爸媽媽甜蜜的說故事時間就要開始囉！

國家圖書館出版品預行編目資料

波波上課記 / Justine Korman 著;Lucinda McQueen
繪;[三民書局]編輯部譯.－－初版一刷.－－臺北
市；三民，民90
　　面;公分－－(探索英文叢書.波波唸翻天系列;3)
中英對照
ISBN 957-14-3442-6　(平裝)
　1.英國語言－讀本

805.18　　　　　　　　　　　　　90003946

網路書店位址　http://www.sanmin.com.tw

© 　波波上課記

著作人　Justine Korman
繪　圖　Lucinda McQueen
譯　者　三民書局編輯部
發行人　劉振強
著作財
產權人　三民書局股份有限公司
　　　　臺北市復興北路三八六號
發行所　三民書局股份有限公司
　　　　地址／臺北市復興北路三八六號
　　　　電話／二五〇〇六六〇〇
　　　　郵撥／〇〇〇九九九八——五號
印刷所　三民書局股份有限公司
門市部　復北店／臺北市復興北路三八六號
　　　　重南店／臺北市重慶南路一段六十一號
初版一刷　中華民國九十年四月
編　號　S 85591
定　價　新臺幣壹佰玖拾元
行政院新聞局登記證局版臺業字第〇二〇〇號

有著作權·不准侵害

ISBN　957-14-3442-6　（平裝）